DOODLE CAT WEARS A CAPE

Published by Scribble, an imprint of Scribe Publications, 2019
18–20 Edward Street, Brunswick, Victoria 3056, Australia
2 John Street, Clerkenwell, London, WC1N 2ES, United Kingdom
3754 Pleasant Ave, Suite 100, Minneapolis, Minnesota 55409 USA

Text © Kat Patrick 2019
Illustrations © Lauren Farrell 2019

9781925713961 (Australian hardback)
9781911617891 (UK hardback)
9781947534988 (North American hardback)

Catalogue records for this title are available from the National Library of Australia and the British Library

scribblekidsbooks.com

DOODLE CAT WEARS A CAPE

Kat Patrick & Lauren Farrell

SCRIBBLE

I am Doodle Cat.

(TEA TOWEL)

Look at my cape!

Isn't it excellent?

My cape gives me
cool superpowers.

I can save a human from a tree!

I can fire furballs at high speed!

PAP!

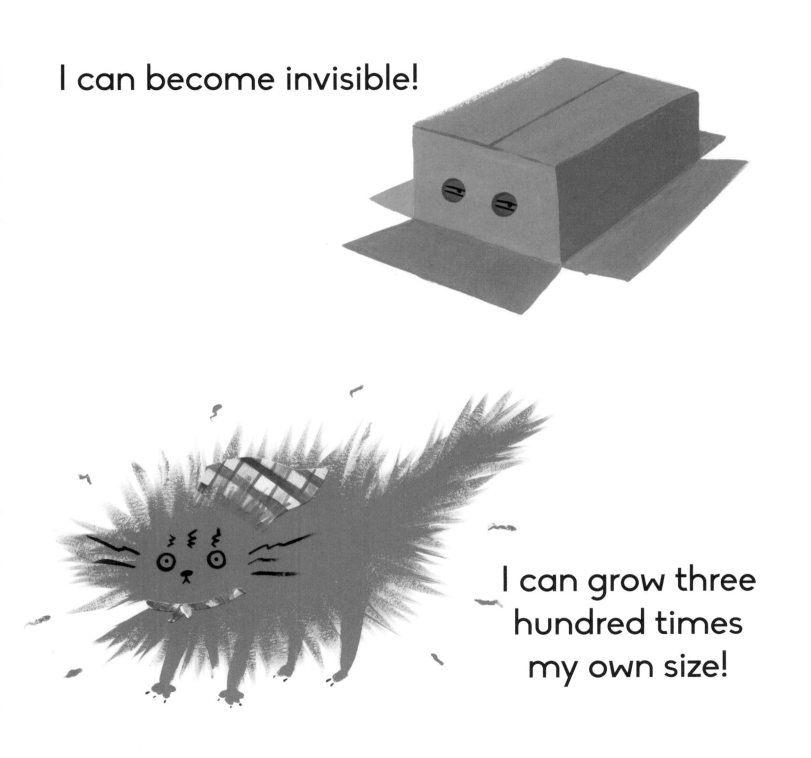

HEY! There's my friend Pangolin.

Pangolin?

Pangolin is sad.

I can use my cool superpowers

to cheer him up!

They aren't working

There is one superpower
I haven't used yet.

Pangolin feels a bit better.

Wait a minute.

Pangolin has cool superpowers too!

You'll need a cape, then!

Pangolin can turn into a rock!

Pangolin can smell everything!

Pangolin can zoom
faster than the
speed of sound!

Pangolin can dig
to the center of
the earth!

Pangolin can lick the Milky Way!

Together we are superfriends.

There are enough capes
for everyone!

I am Doodle Cat. This is Pangolin.

LOOK AT OUR CAPES!

What superpowers do you have?